This book belongs to:

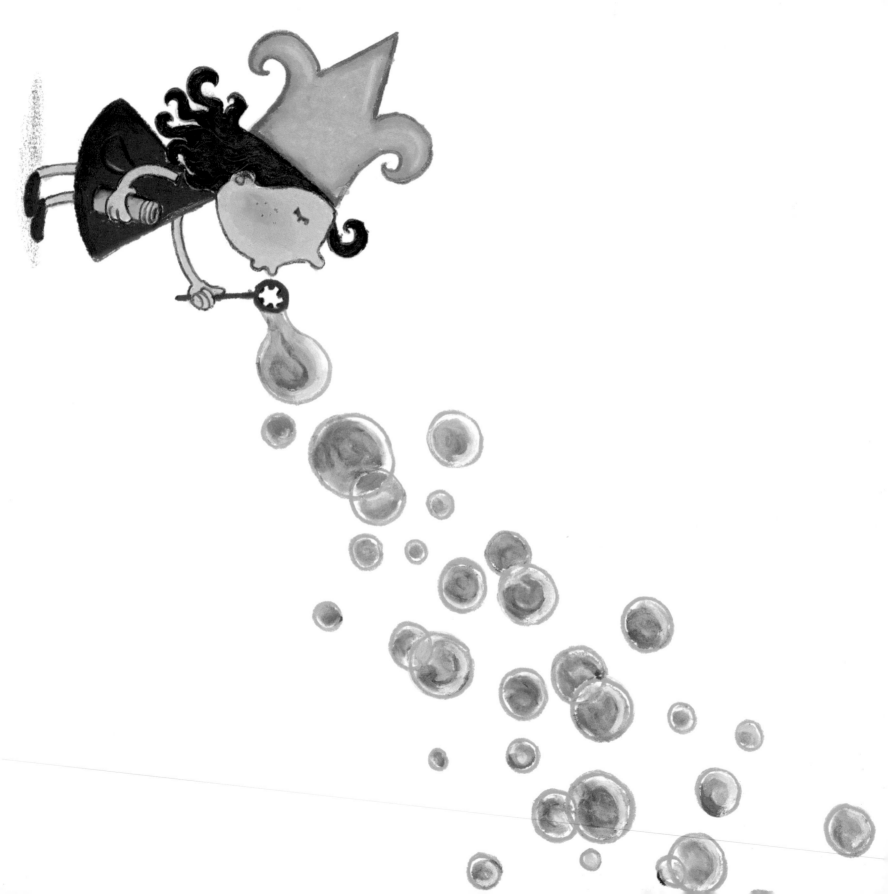

To Yasmin, Amy and all the children
at Longfield First School

DEAR DRAGON
by An Vrombaut
www.vrombaut.co.uk

First published in 2005 by Hodder children's books
First published in paperback in 2009

Text and illustrations copyright © An Vrombaut 2005

Hodder children's books
338 Euston Road, London, NW1 3BH

Hodder children's books Australia
Level 17/207 Kent Street, Sydney, NSW 2000

A catalogue record of this book is
available from the British Library.

ISBN: 978 0 340 88150 7

10 9 8 7

Printed in china

Hodder children's Books is a division
of Hachette children's Books,
An Hachette UK company
www.hachette.co.uk

Dear Dragon

An Vrombaut

h
Hodder
Children's
Books

A division of Hachette Children's Books

Once upon a time there was a dragon.
A dreadful dragon.

DRAGONS ARE
DREADFUL.

ARE YOU BRAVE
ENOUGH TO READ
AND FIND OUT MORE?

DRAGONS

'How dreadful?'
asked Princess Florrie.

'Truly dreadful,'
said the cook.

'Horribly dreadful,'
said the wizard.

'Terrifyingly dreadful,'
said the knights.

'Great,' said Florrie.
'The DREADFULLER the better!'

Just then, Sir Ferdinand arrived.

'Princess Florrie,' he said. 'Tomorrow is your birthday. Would you like a juggler, a jester, or an acrobat at your party?'

'I'm sick of jugglers, jesters and acrobats,' said Florrie.
'I'm too grown up. I want something dreadful, like a...
dragon!' And off she skipped blowing bubbles.

Sir Ferdinand sighed.

He decided to book the juggler

AND the jester

AND the acrobat.

Late at night, when the moon hung over the castle and everyone was fast asleep, Florrie picked up her feather quill and began to write:

Dear Dragon,

I have heard that you are truly, horribly and terrifyingly dreadful.
So please can you come to my birthday party?
(Tomorrow morning in the castle.)

Yours royally,
Princess Florrie

Florrie carefully sealed the letter.

She slid down the tower,
tiptoed through the garden
and walked deep into the wood,
until she arrived at a door.

Knock, Knock!

'WHO IS KNOCKING ON MY DOOR?' called a voice.
'It's me!' said Princess Florrie. 'I'm looking for a
dreadful dragon.'
The door slowly opened. Then there was a crackle and a roar...

'i am the **DREADFULLEST** dreadful dragon!'

'Help!' shrieked Florrie because this dragon was a bit TOO dreadful (even for a brave princess). And so, quick as a flash...

and scrambled to the top of an old mulberry tree.

and dived...

Florrie ducked...

But Florrie
was clever.
'LOOK DRAGON!'
she said,
and she blew
a BIG bubble.

'GOTCHA!' roared the
dragon, with steaming nostrils
and a sizzling tongue.

It floated down and
landed on the dragon's nose.

Now the dragon was cross.
He grabbed the tree and
shook it, harder and harder...

POP!

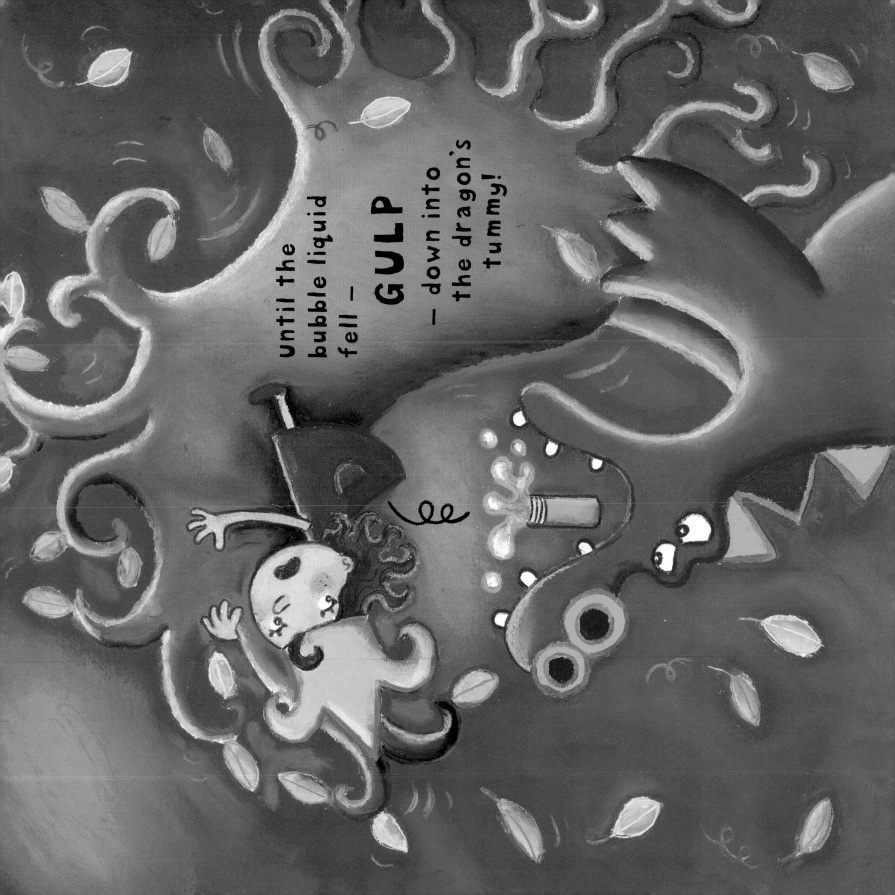

Now the dragon
was very cross!
He opened his mouth
as wide as he could
and... blew a BUBBLE!
'Floundering flames!'
grumbled the dragon.
He tried again and again...
and blew more and
more bubbles.

'What use is
a dragon who
can't blow fire?'
the dragon wailed.
'I'm supposed to
be scary...'

Florrie
climbed down
from the tree.
'I think your bubbles
are lovely,' she said.
'And very useful
too!'

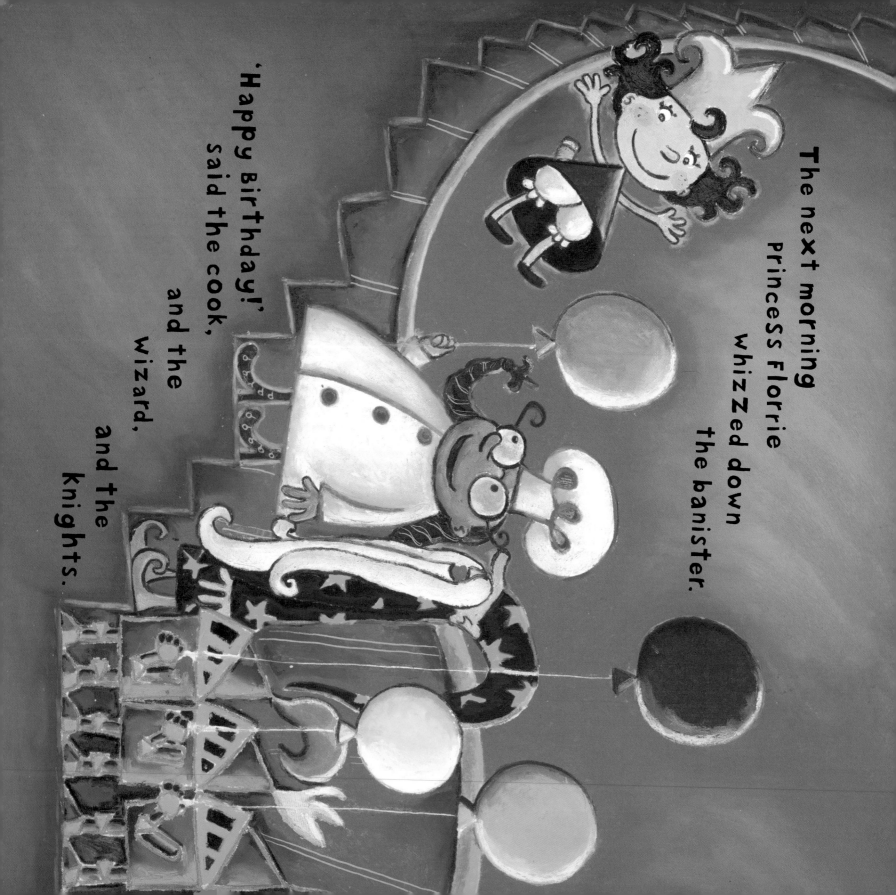

The next morning Princess Florrie whizzed down the banister.

'Happy Birthday!' said the cook, and the wizard, and the knights.

'Princess Florrie!' said Sir Ferdinand, 'you're late for your party. What have you been doing...?'

RRR!'

Everyone shook and
everyone shuddered...

Everyone quaked and
everyone quivered...

'Don't be scared,' said Florrie.
'It's just dear Dragon.'

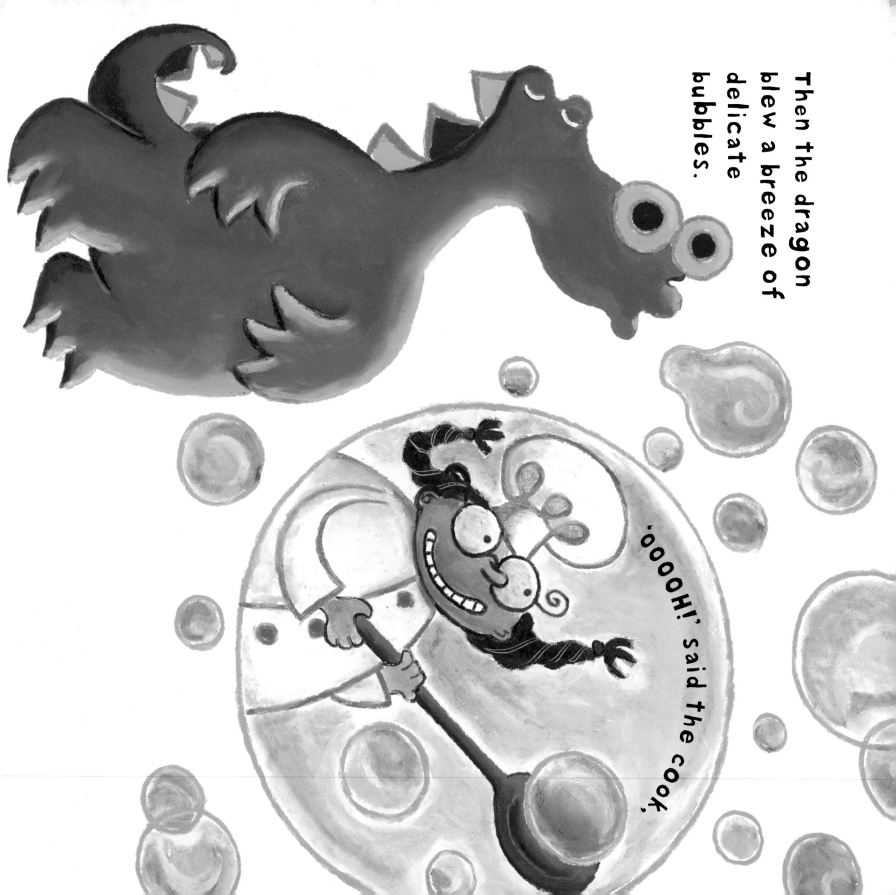

Then the dragon blew a breeze of delicate bubbles.

'OOOOH!' said the cook.

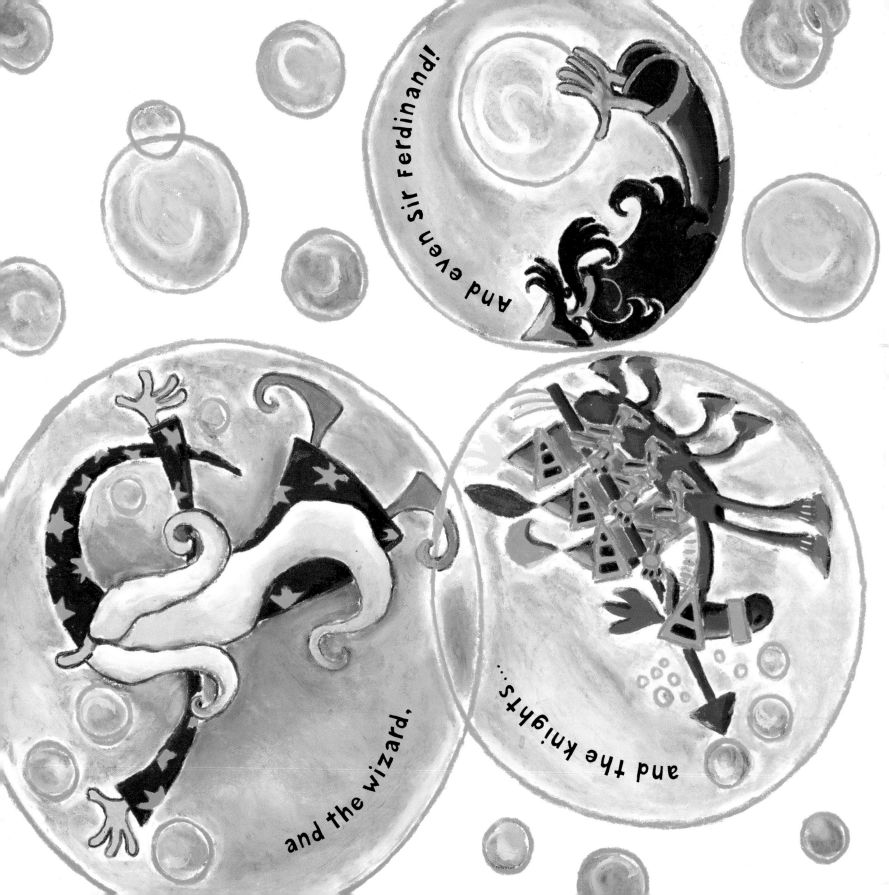

And even Sir Ferdinand!

and the wizard,

...and the knights

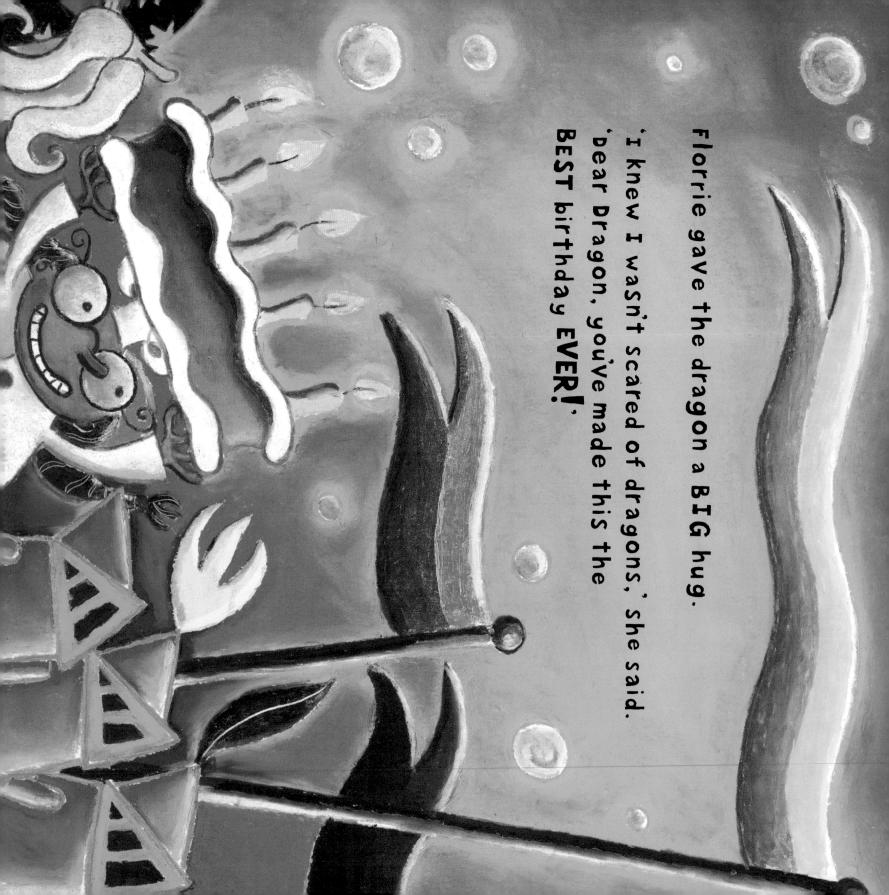

Florrie gave the dragon a BIG hug.

'I knew I wasn't scared of dragons,' she said.

'Dear Dragon, you've made this the BEST birthday EVER!'

Other great picture books by An Vrombaut:

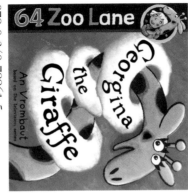

64 Zoo Lane
Georgina the Giraffe
An Vrombaut
based on the television series
978 0 340 78861 5

The Dragon Festival
An Vrombaut
978 0 340 93238 4

64 Zoo Lane
Joey the Kangaroo
An Vrombaut
based on the television series
978 0 340 85560 7

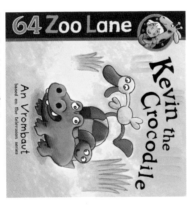

64 Zoo Lane
Kevin the Crocodile
An Vrombaut
based on the television series
978 0 340 79562 0

64 Zoo Lane
Snowbert the Polar Bear
An Vrombaut
based on the television series
978 0 340 78859 2

64 Zoo Lane
Zed the Zebra
An Vrombaut
based on the television series
978 0 340 79560 6

64 Zoo Lane
Henrietta the Hairy Hippo
An Vrombaut
based on the television series
978 0 340 85562 1

Hodder
Children's
Books

A division of Hachette Children's Books